Acting Edition

I0741566

The Gardens of Anuncia

A New Musical by
Michael John LaChiusa

Based on the stories of
Graciela Daniele

ISBN 978-0-573-71150-3

www.concordtheatricals.com
www.concordtheatricals.co.uk

FOR PRODUCTION INQUIRIES

UNITED STATES AND CANADA
info@concordtheatricals.com
1-866-979-0447

UNITED KINGDOM AND EUROPE
licensing@concordtheatricals.co.uk
020-7054-7298

Each title is subject to availability from Concord Theatricals Corp., depending upon country of performance. Please be aware that THE GARDENS OF ANUNCIA may not be licensed by Concord Theatricals Corp. in your territory. Professional and amateur producers should contact the nearest Concord Theatricals Corp. office or licensing partner to verify availability.

No one shall make any changes in this title(s) for the purpose of production. No part of this book may be reproduced, stored in a retrieval system, scanned, uploaded, or transmitted in any form, by any means, now known or yet to be invented, including mechanical, electronic, digital, photocopying, recording, videotaping, or otherwise, without the prior written permission of the publisher. No one shall share this title(s), or any part of this title(s), through any social media or file hosting websites.

For all inquiries regarding motion picture, television, online/digital and other media rights, please contact Concord Theatricals Corp.

THIRD-PARTY MATERIALS USE NOTE

Licensees are solely responsible for obtaining formal written permission from copyright owners to use copyrighted third-party materials (e.g., incidental music not provided in connection with a performance license, artworks, logos) in the performance of this play and are strongly cautioned to do so. If no such permission is obtained by the licensee, then the licensee must use only original materials and materials that the licensee owns and controls. Licensees are solely responsible and liable for clearances of all third-party copyrighted materials, and shall indemnify the copyright owners of the play(s) and their licensing agent, Concord Theatricals Corp., against any costs, expenses, losses and liabilities arising from the use of such copyrighted third-party materials by licensees. For music, please contact the appropriate music licensing authority in your territory for the rights to any incidental music not provided in connection with a performance license.

IMPORTANT BILLING AND CREDIT REQUIREMENTS

If you have obtained performance rights to this title, please refer to your licensing agreement for important billing and credit requirements.

THE GARDENS OF ANUNCIA received its world premiere on September 17, 2021, at The Old Globe (Barry Edelstein, Erna Finci Viterbi Artistic Director; Timothy J. Shields, Managing Director) in San Diego, CA. The performance was directed by Graciela Daniele, with choreography by Graciela Daniele and Alex Sanchez, music direction by Deborah Abramson, sets by Mark Wendland, costumes by Toni-Leslie James, lighting by Jules Fisher and Peggy Eisenhauer, sound by Drew Levy, and orchestrations by Michael Starobin. The production stage manager was Anjee Nero. The cast was as follows:

OLDER ANUNCIA................................. Carmen Roman

YOUNGER ANUNCIA .... Kalyn West

MAMI... Eden Espinosa

GRANMAMA..Mary Testa

TÍA ....Andréa Burns

GRANPAPA / THAT MAN / PRIEST /
    MOUSTACHE BROTHER .... Enrique Acevedo

THE DEER / MOUSTACHE BROTHER .... Tally Sessions

THE GARDENS OF ANUNCIA was produced by Lincoln Center Theater in New York City in 2023. The creative team was the same, and the production stage manager was Thomas J. Gates. The cast was the same, with the following change:

OLDER ANUNCIA.................................. Priscilla Lopez

FOREWORD

THE GARDENS OF ANUNCIA opened on November 20, 2023, at the Mitzi E. Newhouse Theater at Lincoln Center following its world premiere at the Old Globe in 2021, marking the seventh collaboration between the prolific composer/lyricist/librettist Michael John LaChiusa and the iconic director/choreographer Graciela Daniele. This enduring relationship began in 1994 with their first show together at Lincoln Center Theater, *Hello Again*. All their musicals share a unique vision and profound insight into the human condition and *THE GARDENS OF ANUNCIA* is no exception. It's based on Graciela's autobiographical stories of growing up in Argentina in the 1940s under the tyrannical Perón regime. She was raised by a matriarchy of three strongly independent women: her mother, her aunt, and her grandmother. As she put it, "these extraordinary goddesses created me, educated me, loved me and sent me into the world" first to be a ballerina at the Teatro Colón in Buenos Aires, then a soloist at the Opéra de Nice in Europe, next to America as a Broadway dancer, and finally becoming a renowned director and choreographer.

THE GARDENS OF ANUNCIA unfolds in the present on the day Anuncia is to accept her lifetime achievement award (a special Tony Award which Daniele received in 2021). She would much rather tend her beloved garden instead of having to "put on false eyelashes and try to remember which people to thank." She finds immense satisfaction nurturing the anemones, irises, peonies, forsythia, and tomatoes she grows in her backyard. Before the ceremony, Anuncia needs to bury the ashes of her aunt, known as Tía, in the garden. The difficulty of saying goodbye to the last of her relatives releases an outpouring of memories of her childhood with her family. Her vivid recollections summon them back to life in this joyous, poignant show.

Though most of the stories and remembrances in *THE GARDENS OF ANUNCIA* are true to life, LaChiusa takes a bit of theatrical license here and there, for example naming the central character Anuncia instead of Graciela. He explains, "Graciela was born on the Feast of the Immaculate Conception, which is a theological idea. I decided to switch holidays to the Feast of the Annunciation which I think is a powerful tale. The angel Gabriel came to Mary and asked her if she was willing to carry the son of God. Mary was given the choice whether to accept this gift or not." Indeed, many of the real-life events in *THE GARDENS OF ANUNCIA* involve the hard choices made by Graciela's fierce female-centric family in a male-dominated world. The name Anuncia is an apt one for someone who chose to pursue her gift in her own personal way and on her own terms.

This musical is a delight to stage with a cast of five actresses playing women of immense depth and character. The two male cast members have their share of theatrics performing all the men (and a magic realism singing deer).

THE GARDENS OF ANUNCIA is a rarity in twenty-first-century theater, a completely original musical born of a longtime collaboration of two supremely talented and experienced artists. It is also a beautiful act of gratitude from Graciela Daniele to those that formed her and from Michael JohnLaChiusa to his director and cherished friend. It is not a show business story, but it is rich in melody, drama, and imagination. It is an homage to a family of goddesses who thrived despite the odds and a woman who knows that nurturing her garden is necessary to nurturing her art.

Ira Weitzman

Musical Theater Producer, Lincoln Center Theater

CHARACTERS

OLDER ANUNCIA – mid seventies to early eighties

YOUNGER ANUNCIA – plays eight years old to early teens

MAMI (CARMEN) – Anuncia's mother, late thirties

GRANMAMA (MAGDALENA) – Anuncia's grandmother, mother of Carmen and Lucia, early sixties

TÍA (LUCIA) – Anuncia's aunt, sister of Carmen, early thirties

GRANPAPA (ROGELIO) – Anuncia's grandfather, sixties

THE DEER

THE DEER and **GRANPAPA** will double as **SOLDIERS**, and the **MOUSTACHE BROTHERS 1 & 2**.

The two **DEER** are to be played by the same actor.

GRANPAPA will double as **THAT MAN** and the **PRIEST**.

SETTING & TIME

The play takes place in the present in the U.S.A., and in the past (1940s–50s) in Buenos Aires, Argentina, during the Juan and Eva Perón regime.

However, what is present and what is past should be loosely interpreted. Older Anuncia and Younger Anuncia, whether in the past or the present, should freely converse and interact with each other, both in dialogue and staging.

MUSIC NUMBERS

01. Opening . . . . Older Anuncia, Younger Anuncia, Mami, Tía, Granmama

02. Mami Said . . . . Older Anuncia, Younger Anuncia, Mami

02a. Radio Aria . . . . Tía

03. Listen to the Music . . . . Tía, Younger Anuncia

04. Waiting/Dreaming . . . . Granmama, Granpapa

05. Dance While You Can. . . . . Deer, Older Anuncia

05a. Mami's Tango . . . . Instrumental

06. Malagueña . . . . Mami

07. The Annunciation . . . . Tía, Mami, Granmama

08. Smile For Me, Lucia . . . . Brothers 1 &2, Tía

08a. Smile For Me, Lucia (Reprise) . . . . Older Anuncia

09. The Vigil . . . . Older Anuncia, Younger Anuncia, Tía, Granmama, Granpapa, Brother 2

10. The Deer's Story/Dance While You Can (Reprise) . . . . Deer, Older Anuncia

11. Granpapa . . . . Instrumental

11a. Forsythia . . . . Instrumental

12. Travel. . . . . Granpapa, Younger Anuncia

13. Miss The Man . . . . Granmama

14. The Story of That Man. . . . . Mami, Tía, Granmama, Older Anuncia, Younger Anuncia

15. Listen to the Music (Reprise) . . . . Older Anuncia, Younger Anuncia

16. Never A Goodbye . . . . Tía, Mami, Granmama

17. Finale. . . . . Tía, Mami, Granmama, Older Anuncia, Granpapa, Deer

18. Bows/Exit Music . . . . Instrumental

*(Lights on **OLDER ANUNCIA**. She is in her garden. She is dressed simply; in her right hand is a gardening glove. She carries a small box. Her garden is a lovely place, calm and green, with a bench to rest on.)*

[NO. 01 – OPENING]

TÍA.
ANUNCIA!

MAMI.
ANUNCIA!

GRANMAMA.
ANUNCIA!

OLDER ANUNCIA. Okay. Where should I put her? I'd put her in her favorite spot but for some reason the irises are there now – why are you irises growing ten feet from where I planted you last year? You like the sun there, I know.

MAMI.
ANUNCIA!

OLDER ANUNCIA. Today the peonies sound like Mami, which makes sense because peonies were her favorite flower.

GRANMAMA.
ANUNCIA!

OLDER ANUNCIA. And the tomatoes sound like Granmama. She'd tell me, "Don't plant your tomatoes too close together or they'll become resentful. And there's nothing you can do with a resentful tomato."

TÍA.
ANUNCIA.

OLDER ANUNCIA. Tía loved you, my garden. With what's happening in the world these days, you're the only thing that keeps me sane.

TÍA.
ANUNCIA...

MAMI.
ANUNCIA...

GRANMAMA.
ANUNCIA...

OLDER ANUNCIA. *(To the voices:)* Yes, I hear you. I hear all of you.

(Back to her garden:) My first cup of coffee in the morning triggers their laughter. When I wash my face at night, they tell me to "Moisturize, Anuncia, moisturize!" I'm out here weeding and they're warning me about certain beetles. When I bite into a tomato sandwich I can taste them. When I fold laundry, I can smell them... *Ay! Dios mío!* I don't want to go back to the city tonight. I hate award ceremonies. "Lifetime Achievement Award." Ridiculous. Who needs an award for living so long? I'll tell my husband to go in my place, accept this award and I'll get to stay here and not have to put on false eyelashes and try to remember which people to thank.

(A beat.)

Where is my left glove? I'm forgetting things more and more. Because I am too damn old!

Maybe next to the anemones. You anemones are new. I was worried you might not take, especially after that cold snap. But...here you are! *You* deserve a Lifetime

Achievement Award, not I! Since you're new here and don't know me very well, I'll tell you a story that the rest of the garden already knows. Just, please, remind me to water the peonies when I finish.

My so-called father, That Man, left my mother when I was six. My grandmother and Tía, my mother's sister, moved in with us to help raise me since Mami had to find work. This happened in Buenos Aires, in the 1940s, very troubling years in Argentina. Juan and Eva Perón rose to power and we were told to embrace the Fatherland or else. I don't know if I can ever forgive my so-called father for what he did to my mother and me, but if That Man hadn't left us, I wouldn't have had the childhood I had. So, thank God, and to hell with it.

TÍA.
ANUNCIA!
HURRY OR WE'LL BE LATE!

GRANMAMA.
ANUNCIA!
HOW COME YOU MAKE US WAIT?

MAMI.
ANUNCIA!
WHY IS YOUR HAIR SO STRAIGHT?

MAMI, GRANMAMA & TÍA.
AY! WHY IS YOUR HAIR SO STRAIGHT?

YOUNGER ANUNCIA.
EVERY SUNDAY WE WAKE UP EARLY:
MAMI, GRANMAMA, TÍA, AND ME.
WE TRY MAKING MY HAIR STAY CURLY:
MAMI, GRANMAMA, TÍA, AND ME.

YOUNGER ANUNCIA, MAMI, GRANMAMA & TÍA.
WITH A LURCH
WE START UP THE CAR AND DRIVE TO CHURCH.

MAMI.

MASS IS LONG.

TÍA.

BUT THE MUSIC'S NICE.

GRANMAMA.

AND THE WINE IS STRONG.

MAMI, GRANMAMA & TÍA.

COMING HOME, WE BEGIN PREPARING:

YOUNGER ANUNCIA.

MAMI, GRANMAMA, TÍA, AND ME.

MAMI, GRANMAMA & TÍA.

SUNDAY DINNER IS MEANT FOR SHARING.

YOUNGER ANUNCIA.

MAMI, GRANMAMA, TÍA, AND ME.

YOUNGER ANUNCIA, MAMI, GRANMAMA & TÍA.

NEIGHBORS COME:

GRANMAMA.

EAT UP! THERE'S MORE WHERE THAT CAME FROM.

YOUNGER ANUNCIA, MAMI, GRANMAMA & TÍA.

SO MUCH NOISE!

YOUNGER ANUNCIA.

AND I LEARN TO FLIRT WITH THE NEIGHBOR BOYS.

TÍA.

ANUNCIA!
WHAT DO YOU PLAN TO WEAR?

GRANMAMA.

ANUNCIA!
THAT DRESS HAS GOT A TEAR!

MAMI.

ANUNCIA!
WHAT IS IT WITH YOUR HAIR?

MAMI, GRANMAMA & TÍA.
EH? WHAT IS IT WITH YOUR HAIR?
MONDAY'S SCHOOL AND WE HAVE TO HURRY.

OLDER/YOUNGER ANUNCIA.
MAMI, GRANMAMA, TÍA, AND ME.

MAMI, GRANMAMA & TÍA.
CAR WON'T START AND IT GIVES US WORRY.

OLDER/YOUNGER ANUNCIA.
MAMI, GRANMAMA, TÍA, AND ME.

MAMI.
CAR BREAKS DOWN.

GRANMAMA.
AND ALL OF US HAVE TO WALK TO TOWN.

OLDER/YOUNGER ANUNCIA, MAMI, GRANMAMA & TÍA.
IT'S OKAY!

OLDER/YOUNGER ANUNCIA.
WE LAUGH AND SING THE WHOLE LONG WAY.

OLDER/YOUNGER ANUNCIA, MAMI, GRANMAMA & TÍA.
LA, LA, LA, LA, LA, LA, LA, LA, LA!
LA, LA, LA, LA, LA, LA, LA, LA, LA, LA, LA, LA!

> (**TWO PERÓNISTA SOLDIERS** *march on. The* **WOMEN** *suddenly circle around* **YOUNGER ANUNCIA**, *protecting her. The* **SOLDIERS** *spot something offstage and give it chase.*)

SOLDIER. Alto! Alto!

OLDER/YOUNGER ANUNCIA, MAMI, GRANMAMA & TÍA.
LA!

> (**YOUNGER ANUNCIA** *mocks the* **SOLDIERS** *as they run off and* **MAMI** *yanks her back.*)

MAMI, GRANMAMA & TÍA.
TUESDAY MORNING: WE START OUR CLEANING.

OLDER/YOUNGER ANUNCIA.
MAMI, GRANMAMA, TÍA, AND ME.

MAMI, GRANMAMA & TÍA.
WEDNESDAY MORNING: WE STILL ARE CLEANING.

OLDER/YOUNGER ANUNCIA.
MAMI, GRANMAMA, TÍA, AND ME.

MAMI, GRANMAMA & TÍA.
THURSDAY NIGHT:

OLDER/YOUNGER ANUNCIA.
WE KNIT AND WE SEW BY CANDLELIGHT.

MAMI, GRANMAMA & TÍA.
FRIDAY'S HERE.

OLDER/YOUNGER ANUNCIA.
WE SIT ON THE LAWN DRINKING GINGER BEER.

GRANMAMA. I like the ginger beer.

OLDER/YOUNGER ANUNCIA.
JUST US FOUR.
AND NOT ONE MORE.
BUT WHO NEEDS MORE
WHEN FOUR ALL ACT AS ONE?

> *(**YOUNGER ANUNCIA** and **OLDER ANUNCIA** recognize the other, for the first time. It's a shock, then a delight. Throughout the rest of the play, they will connect with each other.)*

ALL WOMEN.
SO WE EKE BY
WEEK TO WEEK.
AND SOMEHOW SQUEAK BY
WHEN THE WEEK IS DONE.

YOUNGER ANUNCIA.
SATURDAY: WE GO MARKET SHOPPING.

OLDER ANUNCIA.
MAMI, GRANMAMA, TÍA, AND ME.

YOUNGER ANUNCIA.
ICE CREAM CONES WITH A CHERRY TOPPING.

OLDER ANUNCIA.
MAMI, GRANMAMA, TÍA, AND ME.

OLDER/YOUNGER ANUNCIA.
THEY WORK HARD.

YOUNGER ANUNCIA.
THEY EACH HAVE A JOB IN THE FISHING YARD.

OLDER ANUNCIA.
I'VE ONE WISH:

OLDER/YOUNGER ANUNCIA.
I WISH THAT THEY DIDN'T SMELL LIKE FISH!

TÍA.
ANUNCIA!
TÍA HAS SEWN YOUR DRESS.

GRANMAMA.
ANUNCIA!
WHO LOVES YOU, CAN YOU GUESS?

MAMI.
ANUNCIA!
WHY IS YOUR HAIR A MESS?

MAMI, GRANMAMA & TÍA.
AY! WHY IS YOUR HAIR A MESS?

OLDER/YOUNGER ANUNCIA, MAMI, GRANMAMA & TÍA.
SUNDAY: DINNER WITH FRIENDS AND NEIGHBORS.
MONDAY: SCHOOL AND THE CAR NEEDS TUNING.

OLDER/YOUNGER ANUNCIA.
TUESDAY MORNING: WE START OUR CLEANING.

MAMI, GRANMAMA & TÍA.
WEDNESDAY MORNING: WE STILL ARE CLEANING.

OLDER/YOUNGER ANUNCIA.
THURSDAY: WORK AND WE SMELL LIKE FISHES.

MAMI, GRANMAMA & TÍA.
FRIDAY NIGHT: AND WE WATCH THE MOON RISE.

OLDER/YOUNGER ANUNCIA.
SATURDAY: WE GO INTO MARKET.

MAMI, GRANMAMA & TÍA.
SOMEHOW WE SURVIVE AND IT'S SUNDAY.

OLDER ANUNCIA.
MAMI, GRANMAMA, TÍA, AND ME!

YOUNGER ANUNCIA.
MAMI, GRANMAMA, TÍA, AND ME!

OLDER ANUNCIA.	**MAMI.**
MAMI, GRANMAMA, TÍA, AND ME!	ANUNCIA!

YOUNGER ANUNCIA.
MAMI, GRANMAMA, TÍA, AND ME!

OLDER ANUNCIA, MAMI & TÍA.	**GRANMAMA.**
MAMI, GRANMAMA, TÍA, AND ME!	ANUNCIA!

YOUNGER ANUNCIA & MAMI.
MAMI, GRANMAMA, TÍA, AND ME!

OLDER/YOUNGER ANUNCIA,	
MAMI & GRANMAMA.	**TÍA.**
MAMI, GRANMAMA, TÍA, AND ME!	ANUNCIA!
MAMI, GRANMAMA, TÍA, AND ME!	

ALL WOMEN.
MAMI, GRANMAMA, TÍA, AND ME!
MAMI, GRANMAMA, TÍA, AND ME!
MAMI, GRANMAMA, TÍA, AND ME!
MAMI, GRANMAMA, TÍA, AND ME!

MAMI. Anuncia! Where is my mascara!

OLDER ANUNCIA. Funny how memories pop up randomly. In surprising ways and unusual places, like you irises.

MAMI. Anuncia!

OLDER ANUNCIA. But are they really memories?

MAMI. Where is my mascara?

OLDER/YOUNGER ANUNCIA. I don't know.

OLDER ANUNCIA. I wonder because sometimes I can change what happened – what happens.

MAMI. Why do you look like a raccoon?

YOUNGER ANUNCIA. I don't know.

MAMI. I told you not to play with my make-up. It's expensive. Do you know how much mascara costs these days?

YOUNGER ANUNCIA. Five-thousand-million-twenty-two pesos.

GRANMAMA. Ay! The sharp tongue on her. Sharp tongues need sharp scissors.

MAMI. Give it to me.

YOUNGER ANUNCIA. I don't have it.

MAMI. Why are you lying?

OLDER ANUNCIA. I'm not lying. Tía borrowed it.

YOUNGER ANUNCIA. Tía borrowed it.

MAMI. You've got mascara all over you!

(**TÍA** *enters.*)

OLDER ANUNCIA. It's mud.

YOUNGER ANUNCIA. I was playing in the creek.

TÍA. Carmen, stop badgering her. I borrowed your mascara.

OLDER ANUNCIA. You see? I changed my memory. Of course, I used Mami's mascara. I ruined the brush and was sentenced to cleaning out the chicken coop for two weeks. To this day, I do not like eggs.

MAMI. Anuncia, I'm going to work now. Did you do your homework?

GRANMAMA. This new job of yours worries me sick. A government job isn't safe, Carmen, you know that.

MAMI. Not in front of the girl, Mami.

GRANMAMA. Why not? She should know her mother doesn't care if her life's in danger every day she walks out that door.

MAMI. It's only a job –

GRANMAMA. People have turned into monsters these days: you don't know who your enemy is anymore. That nice little old man sitting next to you on the bus could suddenly turn you in as a spy – for just half a chicken and a potato!

MAMI. Oh, Mami –

GRANMAMA. Next thing you know they're taking you up in an aeroplane and tossing you out.

MAMI. Not to worry. I keep to myself. The Governor is very nice to me. I smile when I have to; Yes, Sir. No, Sir. Of course, Sir.

GRANMAMA. It's dangerous.

MAMI. It pays well, we have a roof over our heads – and I don't have to smell like the fish market.

(To **YOUNGER ANUNCIA***:)* Did you do your homework?

YOUNGER ANUNCIA. Yes.

MAMI. No, you didn't. You want to grow up to be a dimwit?

YOUNGER ANUNCIA. Yes.

GRANMAMA. The smart mouth on her. Smart mouths have tender bottoms that need a hard spanking.

MAMI. I don't spank.

GRANMAMA. I used to spank you. For all the good it did.

MAMI. My point.

OLDER ANUNCIA. Years later when I graduated from El Theatro Colón Ballet School, I asked Mami if she thought I'd grown up to be a dimwit.

MAMI. I'm very proud of you, you know that. My daughter grew up to become a beautiful ballerina. Illiterate. But beautiful.

OLDER ANUNCIA. I became a dancer by accident.

YOUNGER ANUNCIA. Ouch.

[NO. 02 – MAMI SAID]

MAMI. Why are you limping?

YOUNGER ANUNCIA. My feet hurt.

OLDER ANUNCIA. So we went to the Doctor.

(**MAMI** *and* **YOUNGER ANUNCIA** *go to a doctor.*)

MAMI.
HELP ME, DOCTOR –

OLDER ANUNCIA.
– MAMI SAID.

MAMI.
SHE SAYS THAT HER FEET HURT.

YOUNGER ANUNCIA. My feet hurt.

MAMI.
TELL ME, DOCTOR –

OLDER ANUNCIA.
– MAMI SAID.

MAMI.
> DO YOU KNOW FOR SURE
> IF THERE IS A CURE,
> OR IS IT ALL INSIDE HER HEAD?

> *(She taps* **YOUNGER ANUNCIA***'s head.)*

YOUNGER ANUNCIA. Ouch.

MAMI.
> I'VE HEARD PEOPLE CLAIM THAT BALLET
> CAN STRENGTHEN THE ARCHES, THEY SAY.
> COULD MAKE HER FLAT FEET GO AWAY.

OLDER ANUNCIA.
> AND BEFORE THE DOCTOR COULD GIVE THE OKAY –

MAMI. *(To* **YOUNGER ANUNCIA***:)*
> YOU'RE TAKING A CLASS IN BALLET.

> *(***YOUNGER ANUNCIA** *dances as a little swan
> in Tchaikovsky's "Swan Lake." She performs
> the classic steps quite well – but only for a bit.
> She breaks free and improvises to the music.)*

OLDER ANUNCIA.
> I HAVE TO THANK MAMI FOR THAT.
> IN SPITE OF MY FEET BEING FLAT.
> IT HAPPENED IF ONLY BY CHANCE:
> MAMI TAUGHT ME LOVE FOR THE DANCE.

MAMI. What's wrong with your lip?

YOUNGER ANUNCIA. Got punched at school.

OLDER ANUNCIA. So we went to the school.

MAMI.
> LISTEN, TEACHER –

OLDER ANUNCIA.
> – MAMI SAID.

MAMI.
SHE SAYS THAT SHE'S BULLIED.

YOUNGER ANUNCIA. I'm bullied.

MAMI.
WHY'S THAT, TEACHER?

OLDER ANUNCIA.
– MAMI SAID.

MAMI.
CAN'T YOU SEE SHE'S SMALL
AND NO THREAT AT ALL?
AND NOW SHE'S SCARED TO LEAVE HER BED.

(She elbows **YOUNGER ANUNCIA.***)*

I TAUGHT HER THAT SHE MUSTN'T FIGHT.
BUT NOW THAT MIGHT NOT HAVE BEEN RIGHT.
SHE CAN'T GO THROUGH LIFE IN A FRIGHT.

OLDER ANUNCIA.
AND BEFORE THE TEACHER COULD PONDER MY PLIGHT –

MAMI. *(To* **YOUNGER ANUNCIA***:)*
I'LL JUST HAVE TO TEACH YOU TO FIGHT.

*(***MAMI** *teaches* **YOUNGER ANUNCIA** *to box.)*

OLDER ANUNCIA.
SHE GAVE ME SOME POINTERS AND THEN
I NEVER WAS BULLIED AGAIN.
AND SHOULD I BE UNDER ATTACK,
MAMI TAUGHT ME HOW TO FIGHT BACK.

MAMI. Did you steal money from my purse?

YOUNGER ANUNCIA. *(Yes.)* No.

OLDER ANUNCIA. So we went to the church.

*(***MAMI** *and* **YOUNGER ANUNCIA** *see a* **PRIEST.***)*

MAMI.
BLESS YOU, FATHER –

OLDER ANUNCIA.
– MAMI SAID.

MAMI.
THE GIRL NEEDS CONFESSION.
HELP HER, FATHER.

OLDER ANUNCIA.
– MAMI SAID.

MAMI.
WHEN A YOUNG GIRL SINS
THEN THE DEVIL WINS.
I HOPE YOU'LL SAVE HER SOUL INSTEAD.

(**YOUNGER ANUNCIA** *goes into a confessional booth. It's dark. A* **PRIEST** *is there, cloaked in shadows and with a dark void where his face should be. He speaks from the gloom.*)

PRIEST. What are your sins?

(**YOUNGER ANUNCIA** *trembles – words won't come from her mouth.*)

Tell me your sins.

(**YOUNGER ANUNCIA** *can't speak.*)

I said tell me your sins! You stupid girl – it's your mother's fault, you know. A divorced woman is a disgraced woman. Why are you wasting my time? You want me to box your ears? I'll do it, oh, yes I will!

(**YOUNGER ANUNCIA** *utters a cry of terror and flees from the confessional booth and into the arms of* **MAMI***. The* **PRIEST** *vanishes.*)

MAMI. What?

YOUNGER ANUNCIA. That man scared me.

MAMI. He's a priest. He's supposed to scare you.

> MAYBE I'M NOT BEING FAIR.
> IT'S HARD WITH A FATHER NOT THERE
> TO HELP ME TO RAISE YOU WITH CARE.

OLDER ANUNCIA. Then she whispered as if saying a prayer:

MAMI.

> MAYBE I'M NOT BEING FAIR...

> *(To* **YOUNGER ANUNCIA***:)*

> ALL I HAVE IS YOURS, *MI VIDA*.
> ALL I HAVE TO GIVE.
> YOU'RE THE ONLY REASON
> I WOULD WANT TO LIVE.
> ALL I HAVE IS YOU, *MI VIDA*.
> NO ONE ELSE, IT'S TRUE.
> RIGHT OR WRONG, WHAT I MAY DO,
> I DO FOR YOU.

Can I tell you something, woman-to-woman? I don't believe in God anymore.

But it's fine if you want to. You need to believe in something. Something that matters, something that brings you and others happiness. Like the ballet.

Because when times get tough, and they will, you'll need that thing you believe in to help you get through. Yes?

YOUNGER ANUNCIA. Yes.

MAMI. Let's get out of here. Church always gave me the creeps.

OLDER ANUNCIA.

> SOMETIMES I DOUBT THERE'S A GOD.
> SOMETIMES I PRAY THERE'S A GOD.
> I'M NOT TOO CONCERNED ON THE WHOLE.

OLDER ANUNCIA.
ALL I KNOW IS
MAMI TAUGHT ME I HAVE A SOUL.

[NO. 02A – RADIO ARIA]

(**TÍA** *is sewing and singing to the radio, which is playing a Puccini-like air.*)

TÍA.
HMMM
HMMM
HMMM

YOUNGER ANUNCIA. *(Interrupting.)* Tía, tell me a story.

TÍA. I'm listening to my radio program.

YOUNGER ANUNCIA. Why?

TÍA. Why ask why? Go help Granmama in the garden.

YOUNGER ANUNCIA. It smells like caca.

TÍA. Caca makes the vegetables happy.

OLDER ANUNCIA. I've been in front of an audience since I was a child, and until I was in my thirties, I spent most of my life in front of a mirror perfecting myself. It was liberating to make the transition from dancer to choreographer. When I decided to turn my back to the mirror, I saw before me a world I'd never seen before. And I never looked back at the mirror again. Tía was right. Caca makes the vegetables happy.

TÍA.
HMMM

HMMM

HMMM

HMMM

TÍA. You tell *me* a story.

YOUNGER ANUNCIA. I can't.

TÍA. Everyone can tell a story.

YOUNGER ANUNCIA. How?

TÍA. You're killing me with the questions, Niña.

YOUNGER ANUNCIA. Why?

[NO. 03 – LISTEN TO THE MUSIC]

TÍA. Close your eyes. Now listen…

YOUNGER ANUNCIA. To what?

TÍA.
LISTEN TO THE MUSIC.
TELL ME WHAT YOU'RE SEEING.

YOUNGER ANUNCIA. Nothing.

TÍA.
LISTEN TO THE NOTES
AND LET THEM SWIRL AND DANCE
IN YOUR MIND.
THE PICTURES YOU FIND
ARE LITTLE SEEDS YOU CAN SOW.
LISTEN TO THE MUSIC
AND WATCH YOUR GARDEN GROW.

YOUNGER ANUNCIA. I'm not seeing any garden.

TÍA.
LISTEN TO THE MUSIC.
MAKE BELIEVE YOU'RE FLYING.
FLOATING OVER MOUNTAINS,
THEN YOU STOP TO REST ON A CLOUD.
OF COURSE, YOU'RE ALLOWED
WHATEVER PICTURES YOU SEE.
LISTEN TO THE MUSIC.
AND PLEASE DON'T BOTHER ME.

YOUNGER ANUNCIA. *Tía.*

TÍA.
> MAYBE YOU SEE HORSES:
> GALLOPING WITH THUNDER.
> MAYBE YOU SEE DRAGONS:
> BREATHING FLAMES OF WONDER.
> FOLLOW THE MELODY
> LIKE THE PATH THAT YOU TAKE THROUGH THE PARK.
> AND WHEN IT GROWS DARK,
> YOU CAN FOLLOW IT HOME.
> FOLLOW THE MELODY.
> DON'T BE FRIGHTENED TO WANDER AND ROAM.
> LET IT LEAD YOU.
> LET IT NURSE AND FILL AND FEED YOU!
>
> LISTEN TO THE MUSIC.
> LET THE COLORS FORM INTO SHAPES.
> LIKE PLUMP PURPLE GRAPES,
> THEY'LL MAKE FOR VERY SWEET WINE.
> LISTEN TO THE MUSIC.
> TRY TO SEE THE COLORS.
> TURN THEM INTO PICTURES.
> MAKE THE PICTURES STORIES.
> THEN YOU'LL TELL YOUR STORIES –
> AND I WILL TELL YOU MINE.

YOUNGER ANUNCIA. I see a waterfall!

TÍA. Yes, I see it, too!

YOUNGER ANUNCIA. The water is very blue.

TÍA. And orangey-pink.

YOUNGER ANUNCIA. And polka-dotted!

TÍA. Yes!

YOUNGER ANUNCIA. And over there is a very old tree and its branches are filled with apples and cherries.

TÍA. And cake.

YOUNGER ANUNCIA. Vanilla cake!

TÍA. Deeeeelicious!

YOUNGER ANUNCIA. There's a parade of peacocks coming out of the woods – or maybe they're ostriches – no, they're peacocks, with giant feathers and they're shaking their *culitos*.

TÍA. Shaking their *culitos*?

YOUNGER ANUNCIA. Like this.

(She shakes her culito and **TÍA** *joins in.)*

Look – over there.

TÍA. Where?

YOUNGER ANUNCIA. There, beneath the old tree. There's a man. He's very tired and thirsty and hungry because he's been on a journey.

TÍA. Fetch him a glass of polka-dotted water.

*(***YOUNGER ANUNCIA*** mimes pouring a glass of water.)*

YOUNGER ANUNCIA. He's very handsome.

TÍA. That's good. Where is he traveling to?

YOUNGER ANUNCIA. To his home. And he's been away for a very long time. He misses his family a lot and wants to be with them again. But... I don't know...

TÍA. Niña?

YOUNGER ANUNCIA. My story turned sad.

TÍA. Sometimes that happens. That's okay.

LISTEN TO THE MUSIC.
LISTEN TO YOUR FEELINGS.
DON'T BE SCARED TO HAVE THEM,
GOOD OR BAD, THEY'RE ALL PART OF YOU.

TÍA.
> YOUR STORIES ARE, TOO,
> SO, MAKE THEM STORIES YOU SHARE.
> LISTEN TO YOUR FEELINGS.

YOUNGER ANUNCIA.
> DON'T BE SCARED TO HAVE THEM.

TÍA.
> TURN THEM INTO PICTURES.

YOUNGER ANUNCIA.
> MAKE THEM INTO STORIES.

TÍA.
> SET THEM INTO MOTION.
> MAKE BELIEVE YOU'RE FLYING.
> LISTEN TO THE MUSIC.
> AND DREAM BEYOND A DARE.

> *(**YOUNGER ANUNCIA** and **GRANMAMA** are working in Granmama's garden.)*

GRANMAMA. Don't plant your tomatoes too close together or they'll become resentful. And there's nothing you can do with a resentful tomato.

YOUNGER ANUNCIA. I hate dirt.

GRANMAMA. Dirt is good for you. Everyone should eat a little dirt. Makes you strong.

YOUNGER ANUNCIA. *Ay, Dios mío.*

GRANMAMA. Don't swear.

YOUNGER ANUNCIA. You swear all the time.

GRANMAMA. I'm old. Old people are allowed to swear all the time.

OLDER ANUNCIA. I wonder what Granmama would make of me today, weeding my tomatoes, one missing glove, my nails all dirty. Dancer turned choreographer turned forgetful gardener.

GRANMAMA. Listen to me. Your grandfather comes into port today.

YOUNGER ANUNCIA. Is he coming here?

GRANMAMA. He better not. You go and see him. And ask him for something.

YOUNGER ANUNCIA. What?

GRANMAMA. Ask him for a ham.

YOUNGER ANUNCIA. A ham.

GRANMAMA. I think he sailed to Spain this last trip. Maybe he got a ham.

OLDER ANUNCIA. My grandfather was a merchant marine. Whenever he came back from a voyage, he'd bring me something.

YOUNGER ANUNCIA. If you're married why don't you two live together?

GRANMAMA. Your grandfather values life.

YOUNGER ANUNCIA. But you love him?

GRANMAMA. Of course. I love him very, very much. Ask him for a *smoked* ham.

YOUNGER ANUNCIA. *(To* **OLDER ANUNCIA***:)* Why are old people so confusing?

[NO. 04 – WAITING/DREAMING]

OLDER ANUNCIA. My grandparents were, I suppose you could say, "agreeably separated."

GRANMAMA. I used to be crazy for him. That was back in better days, long before the Peróns and their locusts started chewing up the land. It was like a Feast Day or a birthday party in my heart whenever I said his name: *Rogelio! Rogelio!* Then we got married and that ruined everything. Still, I'd feel so sad when he'd go off to sea, I cried for him every night.

GRANMAMA. I wanted him so much, like my heart was
sliced up and bled out like a poor, little butchered calf.
Love does cruel things like that and that's how you
know it's love.

WAITING THERE AT HOME FOR MONTHS ON END,
BABIES AND A FALLING-DOWN HOUSE TO TEND,
WAITING FOR THE MONEY HE'D FORGET TO SEND,
ALWAYS WAITING.
TWENTY-FIVE YEARS OLD, I LEARNED TO DREAD
EVENINGS CLIMBING INTO AN EMPTY BED,
EVENINGS WANTING HIM SO MUCH IT HURT MY HEAD.
ALWAYS WAITING, WAITING, WAITING.

THEN HE'D COME HOME
WITH HIS STUPID STORIES OF THE SEA;
HE'D DRINK A QUART OF RUM
AND FALL ASLEEP ON ME.
MY HUSBAND WAS A PIG!
WHERE WAS MY DIGNITY?
SUCH DESPAIR!
I HATED HOW HE SMELLED
AND HOW HE CHEWED HIS FOOD.
JUST LOOKING AT HIM
PUT ME IN A ROTTEN MOOD.
I REALIZED OUR MARRIAGE
WASN'T ANY GOOD
WITH HIM THERE.
AND SO:
I KICKED HIM OUT – GOODBYE! BUT STRANGE, SOMEHOW,
THROUGH THE YEARS I WANT HIM MORE THAN EVER NOW.
WHO KNEW THAT I WOULD SAVE
OUR MARRIAGE WHEN I GAVE
HIM THE SHOVE?
THERE'S NO MORE HATING,
JUST CELEBRATING
WHILE I'M WAITING
FOR MY LOVE.

*(*YOUNGER ANUNCIA *is visiting* GRANPAPA.*)*

YOUNGER ANUNCIA. Granpapa!

GRANPAPA. Did you miss me?

YOUNGER ANUNCIA. Yes. Where did you sail to this time?

GRANPAPA. The Mediterranean – where we met with a tremendous storm that almost capsized our ship! Then on to the Canary Islands – *(In a whisper:)* Do you know why they're called the Canary Islands?

YOUNGER ANUNCIA. There are canaries there?

GRANPAPA. No! *(Conspiratorially:)* I'll tell you and you alone: because there are dogs. Hundreds and hundreds of dogs. *Canariae* is the old Latin word for dogs!

YOUNGER ANUNCIA. Can I have a smoked ham?

GRANPAPA. It's really for your grandmother, isn't it?

YOUNGER ANUNCIA. Yes.

GRANPAPA. Does she still wear an onion in her hair?

YOUNGER ANUNCIA. Yes.

GRANPAPA. Crazy woman.

YOUNGER ANUNCIA. If you're married, why don't you two live together?

GRANPAPA. Your grandmother values life.

YOUNGER ANUNCIA. But you love her?

GRANPAPA. There was a time when all I could do was think about her, I'd get so...hot, like the steam that comes out of a bull's nostrils – just saying her name would do that: *Magdalena! Magdalena!* Then we got married and that ended that. But still, when I went to sea, it all would come back: the longing for her – itching and scalding. *That's* how you know it's love.

GRANPAPA.
> DREAMING
> AWAY AT SEA,
> AWAY FROM HER,
> I MISSED HER MORE
> WITH EV'RY MILE BEHIND ME.
> DREAMING
> ONE DAY I'D BE
> BACK HOME WITH HER;
> BUT THEN RETURNING HOME
> WOULD SERVE TO REMIND ME
> WHAT MY LOUSY FATE
> HAD ASSIGNED ME.
>
> STARTING FIRST, SHE'D DISH OUT HER COMPLAINTS.
> I'D BE CURSED IN THE NAMES OF ALL SAINTS.
> THEN THE WORST: SHE WOULD BURST
> INTO TEARS AND SOBBING.
> THEN WE'D FIGHT; OH, SHE GOT IN HER SHOTS,
> OUT OF SPITE, THROWING INSULTS AND POTS –
> NOON 'TIL NIGHT – COME THE LIGHT,
> I'D BE BRUISED AND THROBBING.
>
> THAT'S WHY,
> AWAY AT SEA,
> I HAVE THE WOMAN THAT I'M BETTER OFF
> ONLY DREAMING OF.
> I LOVE MY LAWFUL WIFE.
> BUT IT'S A MUCH LESS AWFUL LIFE
> DREAMING OF MY LOVE.

*(****YOUNGER ANUNCIA**** returns to ****GRANMAMA****.)*

YOUNGER ANUNCIA.   Do you know why the Canary Islands are called the Canary Islands?

GRANMAMA. Lots of dogs there.

YOUNGER ANUNCIA. How come you know that?

GRANMAMA. Your idiot grandfather told me.

> (**GRANMAMA** *and* **GRANPAPA** *sing to – at –
> each other.*)

GRANMAMA.

THAT'S WHY,	**GRANPAPA.**
I KICKED YOU OUT.	THAT'S WHY,
GOODBYE!	
BUT STRANGE, SOMEHOW,	
THROUGH THE YEARS	AWAY AT SEA,
I WANT YOU MORE EVER	
NOW.	
WHO KNEW THAT I	I HAVE THE WOMAN THAT
WOULD SAVE	I'M BETTER OFF
OUR MARRIAGE WHEN I	ONLY DREAMING OF.
GAVE	
YOU THE SHOVE?	I LOVE MY LAWFUL WIFE.
THERE'S NO MORE	
HATING,	
JUST CELEBRATING,	BUT IT'S A MUCH LESS
WHILE I'M	AWFUL LIFE
WAITING FOR –	DREAMING OF –

GRANMAMA & GRANPAPA.

MY LOVE! MY LOVE! MY LOVE! MY LOVE!
MY LOVE! MY LOVE! MY LOVE!

GRANMAMA. When are you leaving again?

GRANPAPA. Next week.

GRANMAMA. *Ay, Díos mío.*

> *(They kiss passionately.)*

OLDER ANUNCIA. I always thought the reason I wasn't
very good at marriage was because of what my so-called
father did to my mother. But I shouldn't blame him,
should I?

OLDER ANUNCIA.   A therapist once told me that if I could reconcile my feelings about That Man, I'd have a more productive life. That was just after I'd opened my twelfth Broadway show. I never saw that therapist again.

> *(The **DEER** appears in **OLDER ANUNCIA**'s garden.)*

DEER. Better weather we've been having.

OLDER ANUNCIA. Yes. Which means you won't have to eat my hedges anymore.

DEER. It was a bad winter. I was hungry. Besides... I like *your* hedges.

OLDER ANUNCIA. It's very funny to me how Americans are so fascinated with what they call "magic realism." In my garden, "magic realism" is just...reality. Flowers float. Tomatoes sing. Deer talk.

DEER. You look blue today.

OLDER ANUNCIA. I have something sad to do, something I've put off for three months. That, and I'm feeling old. It's not fun, this getting-old business.

DEER. Tell me about it. I'm almost five.

OLDER ANUNCIA.   Have you...have you ever had any regrets? In your life, things that you feel guilty about not doing or saying?

DEER. Let me think. *(A beat:)* No.

OLDER ANUNCIA. You are very lucky.

DEER. I could, of course. I could wallow in regret, what would have been, what I should have done: Why wasn't I more honest with my mate? Could I have been a better father?

But it's not healthy to dwell on those kinds of thoughts.

OLDER ANUNCIA. Then you've no conscience.

[NO. 05 – DANCE WHILE YOU CAN]

DEER. Not in your sense of the word. I mean... There are things I won't and don't do. I don't mess with dogs, for instance. I avoid eating soap when used as a deterrent to eating somebody's garden (which doesn't work, by the way). And I try not to cross busy highways, though sometimes I forget. Look: Life can be so easy and beautiful if you *make* it easy and beautiful. Do that and what's to feel guilty about?

> WHAT'S TO FORGIVE?
> WHAT'S TO REGRET?
> THEY'RE ALL FOR NAUGHT,
> THOSE MEM'RIES YOU OUGHT TO FORGET.
> LIVE WHILE YOU CAN.
> LOVE WHILE YOU CAN.
> DANCE WHILE YOU CAN.

OLDER ANUNCIA. My neighbors can see us.

DEER. Where?

> *(He stares out into the audience – a deer in the headlights. Then to her:)*

I'm okay with that.

> IF YOU FEEL SAD
> WHEN YOU'VE DONE WRONG,
> CRY IF YOU MUST,
> BUT DON'T DESPAIR, JUST MOVE ALONG.
> LIVE ALL YOU CAN.
> LOVE ALL YOU CAN.
> DANCE WHILE YOU CAN.
>
> A CONSCIENCE ONLY BOTHERS YOU
> WHEN YOU'RE IDLE.
> THINKING FAR TOO MUCH
> MAKES YOU SUICIDAL.

DEER.

> PUT DOWN THE RAZOR.
> STAY OFF OF LEDGES.
> TEND TO YOUR GARDEN.
> PLANT SOME MORE HEDGES.
> MAYBE YOU'LL FIND –

OLDER ANUNCIA.

> MAYBE I'LL FIND –

DEER.

> SOME KIND OF PEACE.

OLDER ANUNCIA.

> SOME KIND OF PEACE.

DEER.

> LETTING THE PAST BE PAST
> BRINGS YOU LASTING RELEASE.

OLDER ANUNCIA.

> RELEASE!

DEER.

> LIVE AS YOU WILL;
> WILDLIFE OR MAN.
> LOVE WHO YOU WANT,
> AND DANCE, DANCE, DANCE,
> WHILE YOU CAN...

> *(He leads her into a simple, graceful bolero.
> She is as graceful as* **YOUNGER ANUNCIA***.)*

> LIVE AS YOU WILL;
> WILDLIFE OR MAN.
> LOVE WHO YOU WANT,
> AND DANCE, DANCE, DANCE
> WHILE YOU CAN.

> *(***OLDER ANUNCIA** *puts her hands to his face
> to kiss him. But the* **DEER** *gently takes them
> away.)*

DEER. No.

OLDER ANUNCIA. Why not?

DEER. I forgot. I have a dental appointment.

(And he bounds away.)

OLDER ANUNCIA. Weird.

*(**MAMI** appears, dressed to go dancing.
GRANMAMA and **YOUNGER ANUNCIA** are
folding laundry.)*

YOUNGER ANUNCIA. Why do you have to go out?

MAMI. It's my dancing night. You have your ballet class.
I have my tango night.

YOUNGER ANUNCIA. Where do you go?

MAMI. Club Malagueña. Or sometimes to the Casino.
Mostly Malagueña.

GRANMAMA. Filled with Italians. Where she met That
Man, your father.

YOUNGER ANUNCIA. I don't have a father.

GRANMAMA. You do. And he liked to tango, too.

YOUNGER ANUNCIA. Take me with you.

GRANMAMA. It's not for children. And tango is not for
respectable women.

MAMI. Your grandmother is of a different generation.

GRANMAMA. A generation that knows it's a low-life dance
for whores and the low-life men who go to whores.

MAMI. Like your husband?

GRANMAMA. Your father's different. He has mistresses.

YOUNGER ANUNCIA. Teach me.

MAMI. Come, follow me.

[NO. 05A – MAMI'S TANGO]

(**MAMI** *begins dancing a few tango moves and* **YOUNGER ANUNCIA** *mimics her.*)

OLDER ANUNCIA. I have a pair of chipmunks who – every Saturday night – dance the tango, right over there. Very talented *milongueros*. Mami was a *milonguera*, too – every Saturday she went to the clubs in La Boca and danced the tango.

MAMI. You see the patterns?

YOUNGER ANUNCIA. Why do you like the tango?

MAMI. Why do you like the ballet?

[NO. 06 – MALAGUEÑA]

OLDER/YOUNGER ANUNCIA. The feeling of flying.

MAMI. Flying to where?

YOUNGER ANUNCIA. To someplace –

OLDER/YOUNGER ANUNCIA. New.

YOUNGER ANUNCIA. And to fly away –

OLDER/YOUNGER ANUNCIA. *From.*

MAMI. Escape. Yes, that, too.

(**YOUNGER** *and* **OLDER ANUNCIA** *leave* **MAMI** *to her thoughts.*)

THE DAY IS LONG AND BORING.
THE WORK IS DULL AND TRITE.
WHAT HELPS TO KEEP FROM SNORING
IS THINKING OF TONIGHT...
MALAGUEÑA:
THE CLUB ON AZARA STREET.
MALAGUEÑA:
YOU FEEL THAT *MILONGA* BEAT?

WORK'S DONE AND YOU'RE EXCITED,
JUST LIKE A YOUNG GIRL FEELS
WHEN SHE IS FIRST INVITED
TO DANCE IN GROWN-UP HEELS.
MALAGUEÑA:
WHO KNOWS WHAT THE NIGHT WILL BRING?
MALAGUEÑA:
THE NIGHT CAN BRING ANYTHING!

    (Around **MAMI***, Club Malagueña appears, a festive, heated room.)*

AT FIRST YOU WALK THROUGH THE DOOR
AND THE PLACE IS ALIVE
WITH THE CIGARETTE SMOKE
AND THE PINK AND BLUE LIGHTS.
TWO HUNDRED PEOPLE OR MORE –
ALL YOUR PARTNERS ARE THERE:
ESTEBÁN AND LUIS,
AND THE BLONDE – WHAT'S HIS NAME?
THEN YOU STEP OUT ON THE FLOOR
AND YOUR PARTNER TAKES HOLD.
A *CANYENGUE* IS FIRST:
AND YOUR FEET START TO MOVE.
YOU FEEL YOURSELF START TO SOAR,
INTO PINK AND BLUE LIGHTS,
INTO MUSIC AND SMOKE,
INTO LIFE BEYOND LIFE!

    (MAMI *dances to the driving milonga beat. Then:* **THAT MAN** *appears.)*

SOMETIMES YOU MEET THE PERFECT DANCER.
GOOD-LOOKING, CONFIDENT, AND PROUD.
SOMETIMES HE'S QUITE THE FINE ROMANCER.
IT'S OKAY TO BE ROMANCED.
JUST ENJOY IT. IT'S ALLOWED.

*(**MAMI** dances a slow tango with **THAT MAN**. When the tango is finished, **THAT MAN** vanishes.)*

MAMI.

SOMETIMES HE'S JUST A PERFECT DANCER.
THE DANCE IS DONE, AND THEN HE'S GONE.
YOU DON'T ASK WHY; YOU'LL GET NO ANSWER.
IT'S OKAY FOR WHAT IT WAS.
IT'S OKAY THAT YOU MOVE ON...

*(The milonga rhythm returns and **MAMI** is swept up in it again.)*

MALAGUEÑA:
THE CLUB ON AZARA STREET.
MALAGUEÑA!
THE FLUSH AND THE SWEAT AND HEAT,
THE RUSH OF YOUR FLYING FEET,
YOU FEEL THAT *MILONGA* BEAT?
THAT'S LIFE!

OLDER ANUNCIA. Mami... *Mi hermoso misterio.* My beautiful mystery, I called her.

What language do plants understand? I'm guessing English since we're in the U.S. When I came to the U.S., I knew so little English. I *did* know the word "Okay!" I came here, to study jazz dance. A famous choreographer noticed me and offered me a job. I said, "Okay!" Some years later, I was asked to direct my first Broadway musical. I said, "Okay!" If you asked me what would be the title of my memoir, *if* I wrote one – which I won't – I think the title would be "Okay!"

YOUNGER ANUNCIA. *(To **OLDER ANUNCIA**:)* You're putting off what you have to do.

OLDER ANUNCIA. Okay.

(Eva Perón is heard on the radio, making a speech. **MAMI**, **GRANMAMA**, **TÍA**, *and* **YOUNGER ANUNCIA** *are sewing, listening to the radio.)*

GRANMAMA. That woman, Eva – she's the *real* danger. The lies she tells. All those poor people, the *descamisados*, the "shirtless" – they love her. They think she's for them. That she'll make their lives better. Fools. They'll stay as poor as they are while she and her husband get richer off their shirtless backs.

MAMI. Mami, quiet.

TÍA. Eva's a very elegant woman. She speaks from her heart, I think.

GRANMAMA. A snake.

TÍA. Oh, she's doing some good. Helping the children. And women can vote now, thanks to her.

MAMI. Thanks to her, women can vote for her *husband*.

YOUNGER ANUNCIA. I'm changing my name to Eva.

MAMI. No, you're not.

YOUNGER ANUNCIA. It's prettier than "Anuncia."

TÍA. "Anuncia" is just as pretty.

YOUNGER ANUNCIA. Why'd you name me "Anuncia"?

MAMI. You know why.

TÍA. You were born on the Feast of the Annunciation.

YOUNGER ANUNCIA. When Mary got pregnant by Jesus.

MAMI. Pregnant *with* Jesus.

YOUNGER ANUNCIA. *(To* **MAMI***:)* Were you a virgin when you had me?

GRANMAMA. Ha!

MAMI. You know you have a father.

YOUNGER ANUNCIA. I don't have a father.

GRANMAMA. Trust me, you were no virgin birth.

YOUNGER ANUNCIA. I *don't* have a father.

GRANMAMA. Oh, that look she gets in her eyes – you *know* she's That Man's daughter!

YOUNGER ANUNCIA. I'm not! Take it back!

MAMI. Don't talk to your grandmother that way.

GRANMAMA. Oh, those Italian eyes!

YOUNGER ANUNCIA. Tía, you're not married. Does that mean you're a virgin?

TÍA. I try to be.

(*The* **WOMEN** *laugh.*)

YOUNGER ANUNCIA. How can a woman be a virgin *and* get pregnant?

MAMI. That's the miracle, I guess.

TÍA. I like the story of the Annunciation. God doesn't just *make* Mary pregnant. He *asks* her and she gets to decide. Will she become the mother of Jesus and bear all the sorrow that goes with being his mother or will she say no? If she says no, that would mean God wouldn't be able to take human form and live among men. Imagine being a young girl and being handed that burden. I don't know what I'd do.

[NO. 07 – THE ANNUNCIATION]

(*A beat as the* **WOMEN** *consider this.*)

MAMI. If an angel showed up at night by my bedside, I'd scream my head off. Ay!

GRANMAMA. If an angel showed up at night by my bedside,
I'd scream, "Hop on in!"

*(The **WOMEN** laugh.)*

TÍA.
THE WHOLE WORLD WAITED
FOR THE MAIDEN'S "YES."
BUT WHAT SHE'D ANSWER
WAS ANYONE'S GUESS.
THE WHOLE WORLD WAITED
AND IT HELD ITS BREATH
FOR THE MOMENT WHEN LIFE
WOULD CONQUER DEATH.

TÍA & MAMI.
THOUGH SHE WAS CHOSEN,
MARY HAD A CHOICE.
SHE TREMBLED HEARING
THE ANGEL'S SWEET VOICE.
THOUGH SHE WAS CHOSEN,
MARY STILL WAS FREE;
SHE COULD DO AS GOD ASKED
OR SAY, "NOT ME."

GRANMAMA.
THESE DAYS, LIKE THOSE DAYS,
IT'S HARD TO BE A VIRGIN.
WOMEN ALWAYS HAVE TO TAKE CARE.

MAMI.
THESE DAYS, LIKE THOSE DAYS,
THE SLIGHTEST HINT OF SCANDAL
CAN RUIN YOUR LIFE.
SO BEST BEWARE.

GRANMAMA.
SO BEST BEWARE.

TÍA.
SO BEST BEWARE:
IF YOU SHOULD MEET AN ANGEL
TALKING SWEET AND KIND,
WHO OFFERS PARADISE,
KEEP THIS IN MIND:

MAMI, TÍA & GRANMAMA.
THERE'S NO HARM WAITING
TO DECIDE UNTIL
WHAT YOU CHOOSE
COMES FROM YOUR OWN FREE WILL.

MAMI. Free will. I wonder if anyone will have that much longer – if women ever had it to begin with. We have the right to vote, but no choice as to whom to vote for. We're told to "let our voices be heard," but when we speak up, we're told to shut up. Remember, it's the "*Father*land" not the "Motherland." Even Eva Perón has to do her husband's bidding.

YOUNGER ANUNCIA. Mami says she's never getting married again.

MAMI. Never. Once was enough.

YOUNGER ANUNCIA. *(To* **TÍA***:)* Why don't you get married?

TÍA. From what I've seen, getting married doesn't seem a healthy thing to do.

GRANMAMA & MAMI. Oh-ho-ho-ho.

TÍA. I mean, a woman doesn't *have* to get married. She can have a career. Or follow her art.

YOUNGER ANUNCIA. But you like men.

TÍA. Of course. But...I find it hard to take them seriously.

GRANMAMA. Geraldo from the cannery takes *you* seriously.

TÍA. He doesn't have a thumb on his right hand.

MAMI. That's not a missing part you have to worry about, Lucia.

[NO. 08 – SMILE FOR ME, LUCIA]

OLDER ANUNCIA. When she was young, Tía had suitors.

TÍA. The moustache brothers. They both had moustaches. The only way I could tell them apart was by their cars. Oh, they pestered me. Going to church, shopping in the market, waiting for the bus...

> *(The* **MOUSTACHE BROTHERS** *appear.* **BROTHER 1** *begins courting* **TÍA**.*)*

BROTHER 1.
SMILE FOR ME, LUCIA.
HOW ABOUT AN ICE CREAM CONE?
SMILE FOR ME, LUCIA.
ALL I WANT IS YOU ALONE.
WE COULD TAKE A RIDE IN MY CHEVY.
IT'S A BIG AMERICAN CHEVY.
DRIVE INTO THE HILLS AND ON A LARK,
FIND A QUIET PLACE TO PARK;
WATCH THE TWILIGHT FADE TO DARK,
AND LOVE COULD SPARK IN A WHILE.
SAY YES TO ME, LUCIA –
AND SMILE.

BROTHER 2.
SMILE FOR ME, LUCIA.
WOULD YOU LIKE A *CHOCOLAT*?
PLEASE PICK ME, LUCIA.
WHAT YOU WANT IS WHAT I'VE GOT.
WE COULD RACE THROUGH TOWN IN MY CITROËN
IT'S A NEW PARISIAN CITROËN.
DINE WITH *MES AMIS* AT CHEZ MAXINE.
FEAST ON *CHARTREUSE D'AUBERGINE*.
TRUST ME, IT'S *TOUJOURS DIVINE* –

BROTHER 2.
> BY THAT, I MEAN IT HAS STYLE.
> SAY YES TO ME, LUCIA!

BROTHER 1.
> LUCIA!

BROTHER 2.
> LU-CI-HEE-HEE HA HA HA!

BROTHER 1.
> LU-CI-HEE-HEE HA HA HA!

BROTHER 2.
> SMILE FOR ME, LUCIA!

BROTHER 1.
> LUCIA!

BROTHERS 1 & 2.
> LUCIA!

TÍA.
> BASTA!

> *¡¡¡Fuera carajo!!!*

>> *(The* **BROTHERS** *beat a hasty retreat.)*

> *(A beat, a sigh:)* Men can be such children.

>> *(With a flip of her hair and a wise smile, she exits.)*

[NO. 08A – SMILE FOR ME, LUCIA (REPRISE)]

OLDER ANUNCIA. When I last visited Tía, she was smiling, as usual. The nurses told me that sometimes her disease causes a person to revert to a truer self, the person he or she really is, the true person that's been masked or covered over or hidden. Some become naughty like children or dangerous to themselves and others. It's sad, you know? But it's poignant, too. That, even in all its destructive ways, the disease reveals one to be as one really is. Tía is...was...an angel revealed.

SMILE FOR ME, LUCIA...

> (**YOUNGER ANUNCIA** *points to a spot in* **OLDER ANUNCIA**'s *garden.*)

YOUNGER ANUNCIA. You've held onto her ashes for three months. You put it off for too long. Here. This is the spot. She'll like it here.

OLDER ANUNCIA. Will she?

YOUNGER ANUNCIA. The view is better here.

> (**YOUNGER ANUNCIA** *joins* **MAMI**, *who is in Granmama's garden, picking beans.*)

MAMI. Stop daydreaming, Anuncia, or we'll never finish.

YOUNGER ANUNCIA. I hate beans.

MAMI. You love beans.

YOUNGER ANUNCIA. I hate *picking* beans.

MAMI. What's with you today?

YOUNGER ANUNCIA. I've decided something and you can't change my mind. I'm never getting married.

OLDER ANUNCIA. You will. Three times.

YOUNGER ANUNCIA. *(To* **OLDER ANUNCIA**:) No. I won't.

OLDER ANUNCIA. Three times. The third time will be the proverbial charm.

YOUNGER ANUNCIA. *(To* **MAMI**:) I'm never getting married.

MAMI. Who said you had to? Besides, you've got other things to think about now: your ballet –

YOUNGER ANUNCIA. – I'm not going to ruin my life by getting married.

MAMI. Getting married won't ruin your life.

YOUNGER ANUNCIA. Look at what happened to you.

OLDER ANUNCIA. There are times I can't change a memory. I try, but it is too true, too strong to change.

YOUNGER ANUNCIA. Well? Look at what That Man did to you!

OLDER ANUNCIA. Wicked child. Stop it.

YOUNGER ANUNCIA. You married a no-good Italian.

MAMI. Anuncia –

YOUNGER ANUNCIA. That's what Granmama calls him. I hope he's dead wherever he is.

MAMI. Your father is your father wherever he is.

YOUNGER ANUNCIA. Why do you stand up for him?

MAMI. *Anuncia.*

YOUNGER ANUNCIA. You are a hypocrite.

MAMI. What?

YOUNGER ANUNCIA. A hypocrite. You say one thing and do another. You are two things. You hate That Man but you won't let *me* hate him. You hate the government but you *work* for the government. You are two things and that's being a hypocrite.

MAMI. *(Losing her temper.)* I do everything in my power to give you a good, safe life: clothes, food, a home! Your school! Your ballet! I do everything in my power to make you happy and if that means sometimes I have to compromise – if that means I can't be happy – that I can't have –

(**MAMI** *stifles a cry.*)

YOUNGER ANUNCIA. I'll never be as stupid as you.

(A beat. **MAMI** *brushes off her hands.)*

OLDER ANUNCIA. Wicked child. Apologize. Apologize before she leaves.

MAMI. *(Composing herself.)* The car's broke down again. I'll walk to the market to do the shopping. Tell Tía and Granmama where I've gone. I'll be home before six.

(She exits.)

OLDER ANUNCIA. She wasn't back at six. Or at seven. Or at eight.

OLDER/YOUNGER ANUNCIA. Or at nine.

*(***TÍA*** *and* ***GRANMAMA*** *enter, in sheer panic.)*

GRANMAMA. What do you mean she's been arrested?!

TÍA. She was picked up by the police when she was walking back from the market!

GRANMAMA. Why?!

TÍA. I don't know!!

GRANMAMA. Where did they take her?!

TÍA. Oh, Mami...they took her to the prison.

[NO. 09 – THE VIGIL]

GRANMAMA. *(A beat of horror, then mobilizing.)* Lucia, get your father – he's sailing to Europe this Friday – tell him to stay. And Lucia – find out where the girl's father is. We'll need That Man's money. I'll go to the Governor's house – he might be able to pull some strings.

OLDER/YOUNGER ANUNCIA.
MINUTES TURN TO HOURS
AND HOURS INTO DAYS.
WEEKS GO BY AND NOTHING IS DONE.

TÍA & GRANMAMA.
DIOS TE PROTEJA.

OLDER/YOUNGER ANUNCIA.
ALL OF US KEEP BUSY
WHILE MOVING THROUGH A HAZE;
MOVING BUT TOO SCARED TO MOVE ON.

TÍA, GRANMAMA & BROTHER 2.
DIOS TE AMPARE.

OLDER/YOUNGER ANUNCIA.
LETTERS GO UNANSWERED
AND OUR PHONE CALLS ARE IGNORED.
THE GOVERNMENT OFFICIALS
ACT INDIFFERENT OR BORED.
IT'S AS THOUGH THE WOMAN VANISHED
INTO ETHER, INTO AIR.
BUT THEN, HOW CAN PEOPLE VANISH?
ISN'T EV'RYONE SOMEWHERE?
SOMEWHERE... SOMEWHERE...
WEEKS TURN INTO MONTHS
AND WE HAVEN'T HEARD A WORD.
I'M SCARED I WON'T REMEMBER HER FACE.

TÍA, GRANMAMA, GRANPAPA & BROTHER 2.
DIOS TE AYUDE.

OLDER/YOUNGER ANUNCIA.
HOW CAN PEOPLE VANISH?
THE THOUGHT OF IT'S ABSURD.
YET THEY DO, THEY DO WITHOUT A TRACE.

TÍA, GRANMAMA, GRANPAPA & BROTHER 2.
DIOS TE AYUDE.

OLDER/YOUNGER ANUNCIA.
I'M SCARED I WON'T REMEMBER HER FACE.
I'M SCARED I WON'T REMEMBER HER FACE.

(**GRANPAPA** *has a sack of food, preparing to leave for the prison.*)

GRANPAPA. I'm going to try again to get food to Carmen. I think I've found a guard who'll help – for a price.

YOUNGER ANUNCIA. What if she –

GRANPAPA. *Niña*, she will come home. Whatever she's accused of, Carmen did what she believed she should do. Your mother is brave. She has steel. And you have it, too. You remember that, okay?

> DON'T FORGET WHO GAVE YOU
> YOUR IRON WILL AND STRENGTH
> WHEN YOU'RE FEELING SCARED AND ALARMED.
> DON'T FORGET WHO'D BATTLE
> AND GO TO ANY LENGTH
> JUST TO SEE YOU SAFE AND UNHARMED.

YOUNGER ANUNCIA.
> I'M SCARED I CAN'T REMEMBER HER FACE.

OLDER ANUNCIA. It was the end of days for the Perón government; no one was safe. Mami was arrested for what they called "suspicious behavior" and for supposedly passing on information to the opposition forces. I would never learn if she was innocent or not. Would she risk losing her life, even risking her child's life for her beliefs? A mystery.

YOUNGER ANUNCIA. That Man –

OLDER ANUNCIA. That Man who abandoned us, who had the money to help –

YOUNGER ANUNCIA. – That Man does nothing.

OLDER ANUNCIA. After three months, Mami was released from prison and finally came home. She was not the same woman. Not broken – Mami could never be broken. But she never went to La Boca to dance the tango again. And I would no longer be a child.

GRANMAMA. Anuncia, when your mother comes in, don't get too excited – we don't want to upset her after all she's been through. She'll be very tired and she won't want you to be crying or yelling or causing a scene. Do you hear me, Anuncia?

> *(***TÍA*** *enters with* ***MAMI.*** ***MAMI*** *opens her arms to* ***YOUNGER ANUNCIA.****)*

MAMI. Anuncia...

YOUNGER ANUNCIA. Mami...

> *(***YOUNGER ANUNCIA*** *runs into her embrace.)*

GRANMAMA. *(Shrieking.) Ay! Dios Mío! Estás en casa! Sangre de Christo!*

OLDER ANUNCIA. Mami gave me dance. Tía, the gift of music. But I think it was Granmama who gave me my flair for dramatics.

GRANMAMA. *(Offstage.) Ay! Dios Mío!*

OLDER ANUNCIA. When I think about my career – which is not very often – but when I do and remember all the brilliant directors and genius producers and crazy composers I've worked with, I can say this: the theatre has given back to me maybe not so much as I have given it, but it has been rewarding – although I say with every show I start work on that that one will be my last. No more! I am retiring! It seems I've been retiring for decades now. Although I love the theatre, I hate show business.

> *(The* ***DEER*** *is in her garden.)*

Hello again.

> *(The* ***DEER*** *stares at her blankly.)*

Did you come back for another dance?

(A beat.)

DEER. Do I know you?

OLDER ANUNCIA. Of course. You were just here. We danced a *bolero*.

DEER. Oh…that's probably my brother.

OLDER ANUNCIA. Your brother? My deer is your brother?

DEER. Is, was. He's dead.

OLDER ANUNCIA. What happened to him?

DEER. Ran into traffic on the turnpike.

OLDER ANUNCIA. That's terrible!

DEER. He always thought the "deer crossing" signs were meant for deer. Knucklehead.

OLDER ANUNCIA. I'm very sorry.

DEER. For what?

OLDER ANUNCIA. For you. For your brother. You're not sad?

DEER. Why?

OLDER ANUNCIA. He was your brother! Didn't he mean something to you?

DEER. You know I'm a deer, don't you?

OLDER ANUNCIA. Yes, but…your brother was a very nice deer. A very good listener. And sensitive. You're not very much like him.

DEER. Different mothers. You growing any nasturtium?

OLDER ANUNCIA. Your brother was a very good dancer.

DEER. Yeah, yeah, we called him "The Hoofer."

OLDER ANUNCIA. He also had a very good philosophy about the world and of life. Healthy and positive.

DEER. Yeah, sure. What's in the box?

OLDER ANUNCIA. My aunt's ashes.

DEER. Okay. That's disgusting. Can I see?

OLDER ANUNCIA. No! I'm going to bury her. Here in my garden. It's the hardest thing I've ever had to do.

DEER. Bury her. Here? Where I feed?

OLDER ANUNCIA. Oh, never mind. You're a cynic – and a pessimist.

DEER. I'm a nothing-ist. Look, lady, I don't want to get all existential on you, but this business of life? It's meaningless. Look at my brother: one minute he's dancing and leaping about and next minute: Blam! He's a mile-long streak of guts and gore on the highway! What's the meaning of *that*?! Life's just one friggin' prickly pear, lady.

OLDER ANUNCIA. But it doesn't have to be. Your brother told me, "Life can be so easy and beautiful if you make it easy and beautiful."

DEER. He didn't have it as bad as I did. He had talent. Good home. A decent, proper education. Me? Well, I won't bore you with the details of my sorry life.

OLDER ANUNCIA. I understand. And it *is* getting late –

DEER. When I was two,

[NO. 10 – THE DEER'S STORY/DANCE WHILE YOU CAN (REPRISE)]

my father left Ma for another doe – yeah, I know, tough nuggets – but I never saw him again and it hurt, hurt bad. Then you human types built your lousy mall smack on top of what had been our home – no one warned us – and now there's a Chuck E. Cheese where I used to sleep. That left Ma and me homeless, barely scrapin' by. She had to work the stag party circuit just to keep me fed. I offered to sell myself to a petting zoo, but she wouldn't have that, bless her heart. Then she caught a bad case of the Lyme disease and that was that. On the day she died, I didn't cry, no, I did not. I'd used up all my tears. By the time I was three, I was in rough shape – runnin' with a bad herd from Jersey and I was in some deep trouble. Breakin' into homes, destroyin' property, chasin' after every piece of tail in the forest, tryin' to fill a void that could never be filled. Thought of cuttin' out of here, to get a fresh start, a new life in L.A. Get into the movies, live animation work, why not? But a near fatal encounter with an electric fence outside of Scranton put an end to that. It sobered me up but by then I realized the futility of my existence. So, no one's gonna sell me on the meanin' of life, lady, cuz I have learned the sad, sorry truth!

LIFE IS ONLY SMOKE AND MIRRORS.
DON'T TELL ME THAT THERE'S SOME COSMIC REASON
WHEN EV'RY SINGLE DAY IS FRIGGIN' HUNTIN' SEASON!
WHAT A PRICKLY, PRICKLY PEAR –

> (**OLDER ANUNCIA** *suddenly takes him by the hooves.*)

OLDER ANUNCIA.
WHAT'S TO FORGIVE?
WHAT'S TO REGRET?
THEY'RE ALL FOR NAUGHT,
THOSE MEM'RIES YOU OUGHT TO FORGET.
LIVE AS YOU WILL.
WILDLIFE OR MAN.
LOVE WHO YOU WANT
AND DANCE, DANCE, DANCE
WHILE YOU CAN!

> (*The* **DEER** *is so enthralled, he leans in to kiss* **OLDER ANUNCIA**. *She pulls away.*)

No!

DEER. Why not?

OLDER ANUNCIA. You are not my type of deer.

DEER. *(A beat.)* Weird.

> *(He leaps off.)*

[NO. 11 – GRANPAPA]

OLDER ANUNCIA. Would Tía mind if I haven't given her a proper funeral? I never much liked funerals. I remember when Eva Perón died. Thousands of people filled the streets and thousands of flowers showered down from the rooftops – within a day all of the flower shops in Buenos Aires had run out of stock. The country put on quite a show. You can always count on fascists to turn even funerals into spectacular theatre.

> **(YOUNGER ANUNCIA, MAMI, TÍA,** *and* **GRANMAMA** *are gathered around* **GRANPAPA.** *He is on his deathbed.)*

MAMI. Anuncia. Say your goodbyes to your grandfather.

GRANMAMA. And say a prayer his soul will go to Purgatory.

YOUNGER ANUNCIA. Why wouldn't he go to heaven?

GRANMAMA. That's asking too much. He'll like Purgatory. He has friends there.

TÍA. He's dying, Anuncia. Say your goodbyes.

> **(MAMI, GRANMAMA,** *and* **TÍA** *exit.)*

YOUNGER ANUNCIA. Goodbye, Granpapa.

> **(OLDER ANUNCIA** *tosses a handful of forsythia in the air over* **GRANPAPA.**)*

[NO. 11A – FORSYTHIA]

OLDER ANUNCIA. Forsythia!

YOUNGER ANUNCIA. Forsythia?

(Suddenly, **GRANPAPA** *leaps from the bed, in good, healthy form.)*

GRANPAPA. Ha! Forsythia!

OLDER ANUNCIA. They say it's a temporary restorative.

GRANPAPA. Come closer. Look at you! How fast life happens! Yesterday, a child; today, a young woman. Tell me: what have you been up to?

YOUNGER ANUNCIA. I've been hired as a soloist to dance for Teatro Argentino.

GRANPAPA. That's wonderful! This is a happy day for you!

YOUNGER ANUNCIA. It's not. I'll never see you again –

GRANPAPA. Hush – or I won't give you the present I have for you.

YOUNGER ANUNCIA. What present?

GRANPAPA. This is a magical scarf

[NO. 12 – TRAVEL]

spun from the silk threads of a thousand caterpillars and once worn by a Chinese princess who had the most luminous eyes and lips as soft as cherry blossoms. She gave it to me as a parting gift after a blissful, though strenuous, evening in Shanghai – don't tell your grandmother. And now that you are a young woman, you will need this magical scarf as you begin your many journeys.

YOUNGER ANUNCIA. But I'm not going anywhere.

GRANPAPA. Oh, but you will, young lady, you will!

THE TREASURES OF THE WORLD AWAIT YOU.
SUCH WONDERS TO BE FOUND.
ITS PLEASURES WILL INTOXICATE YOU:
ITS MYSTERIES ABOUND.

GRANPAPA.
> FROM THE STRAITS OF GIBRALTAR
> TO THE RUINS OF TIMBUKTU,
> IN THE WILDS OF NEW GUINEA,
> ON THE SLOPES OF KATHMANDU.
> THE WORLD WILL AWE AND FASCINATE YOU,
> EV'RY SIGHT AND EV'RY SOUND.
> TRAVEL!
> TRAVEL!
> START WHILE YOU ARE YOUNG.
> NOW WHEN YOU HAVE EYES TO SEE
> AND TASTEBUDS ON YOUR TONGUE.
> CROSS THE OCEANS.
> TAKE IN THE BRINY FOAM.
> GATHER UP THE WORLD TO YOU
> AND BRING THE WORLD BACK HOME.

> *(**GRANPAPA** removes the scarf from around
> his neck. It is very, very long. He enfolds his
> granddaughter in it.)*

YOUNGER ANUNCIA. That's why you shouldn't die. Who's
going to bring me things from wherever you've been?

GRANPAPA.
> THAT IS WHY *YOU* MUST – TRAVEL!

YOUNGER ANUNCIA.
> TRAVEL!

GRANPAPA.
> TRAVEL!

YOUNGER ANUNCIA.
> TRAVEL!

GRANPAPA.
> TEST HOW FAR IS FAR.

YOUNGER ANUNCIA.
> TEST HOW FAR IS FAR.

GRANPAPA.
ANYWHERE IS HOME

GRANPAPA & YOUNGER ANUNCIA.
IF YOU'RE IN LOVE WITH WHERE YOU ARE.
SCALE GREAT MOUNTAINS.

GRANPAPA.
IT'S WHAT YOU'RE MEANT TO DO.

YOUNGER ANUNCIA.
WHAT I'M MEANT TO DO.

GRANPAPA.
GO AND FIND THE WORLD
AND YOU WILL FIND THE WORLD IS YOU.
FAREWELL, MY LOVE, THERE'S NO MORE STALLING.
I LEAVE WITHOUT DELAY.
FAREWELL, MY LOVE, ADVENTURE'S CALLING,
AND I MUST SAIL AWAY.
PAST THE PEAKS OF THE ANDES
INTO NEW, UNCHARTED SKY.
'ROUND THE SMILE OF THE FULL MOON,
BEYOND THE RINGS OF SATURN,
T'WARD THE LIGHT OF THE PLEIADES,
INTO THE ARMS OF THE UNIVERSE,
I'LL FLY!

GRANPAPA & YOUNGER ANUNCIA.
AND
TRAVEL!
TRAVEL!
TRAVEL!

GRANPAPA. *(Tenderly.)* Goodbye.

*(**GRANPAPA** departs.)*

GRANMAMA. Eat your macaroni.

YOUNGER ANUNCIA. I'm not hungry.

GRANMAMA. There are children all over the world starving for macaroni. Poor children in places that don't know how to *make* macaroni. Those poor, starving children would die for a plate of your macaroni.

YOUNGER ANUNCIA. I'm not a child anymore. If I don't feel like eating, I don't have to.

GRANMAMA. You're sad about your grandfather. You miss him? I don't. There are people all over the world starving for what I had. I had a belly full of him.

I will tell you the story of how your grandfather and I got married. My family was very poor so I was sent to work as a maid in the very big house of a very rich family. A family of all sisters, except for the youngest child, a handsome young man. Guess who he was and guess who fell in love with the maid?

YOUNGER ANUNCIA. Granpapa.

GRANMAMA. *(With a sigh:)* His two strong arms felt like a thousand arms around me... Now, it would have been big trouble if your grandfather and I were to be found out by his sisters. We had to take care and be very secretive where and when we met. So, when the coast was clear, and all the sisters were either out shopping or in church or taking a siesta, I would snitch an onion from the pantry, put it in my hair, run up to the floor where his bedroom was, and roll the onion down the hallway. When he saw it, he'd know it was safe for us to grab a moment alone together – in the wine cellar, or in a closet. Eventually we were found out: the cook discovered that I'd been stealing hundreds of onions! How his sisters hated me. Imagine their little darling prince in love with a little mongrel maid – yes, a mongrel. My father was Italian. Don't look so shocked! There's no such thing as a pure race and if anyone claims there is, don't believe it. How that family hated me even more after your grandfather asked me to marry him. Well. Things were never as good or as passionate after that. I tell you, secret love is the best love of all.

YOUNGER ANUNCIA. I'm sad for you then. Now you're going to be all alone.

[NO. 13 – MISS THE MAN]

GRANMAMA. Alone? I have my daughters. I have you. I have myself.

SHOULD I MISS THE MAN?
SHOULD I MISS HIS VICES?
SHOULD I MISS HIS FLAWS?
HIS DIRTY NAILS AND SMELL OF CHEAP COLOGNE?
SHOULD I MISS THE MAN?
WOULD HE NEED MY TEARS?
WITH ALL HE PUT ME THROUGH,
WHAT GOOD WOULD CRYING DO?
WHAT GOOD FOR ALL THESE
YEARS AFTER YEARS AFTER YEARS?

I COULD MISS THOSE MOMENTS
TOO SHORT AND TOO RARE.
A KISS KISSED IN SECRET
OR JOKE THAT WE'D SHARE.
THOSE ONE OR TWO MOMENTS
WHEN I CAME TO SEE
THAT SOMEONE HAD BEEN PUT ON EARTH
JUST FOR ME.
THOSE ONE OR TWO MOMENTS THAT I CAN'T REGRET.
EVERYTHING ELSE MAY BE BEST TO FORGET.

IF I MISS THE MAN,
WOULD THAT MAKE ME LONELY?
SHOULD I MISS THE MAN,
YOU MUSTN'T WORRY, I CAN BE ALONE.
SOMEDAY YOU WILL LEARN
THE LONGER THAT YOU LIVE

GRANMAMA.
>HOW HARD IT IS TO LOVE;
>AND YET, IF YOU KNOW LOVE,
>HOW EASY TO FORGIVE AND FORGIVE
>AND FORGIVE.
>
>EAT YOUR MACARONI.
>I DON'T WANT YOU STARVING.
>I DON'T EVER WANT YOU STARVING...

>>(**GRANMAMA** *begins to unwind an imaginary onion from the bun of her hair. She rolls the onion across the floor. A* **MAN***'s hand catches it. A pair of arms reach out to her.* **GRANMAMA** *smiles and walks toward and into the open arms of her lover.*)

>>(*The sound of a distant explosion.* **MAMI** *and* **YOUNGER ANUNCIA**.)

MAMI. Get away from the window.

YOUNGER ANUNCIA. There's smoke – must be coming from the Plaza –

MAMI. Anuncia! We'll pack what we can carry and get out of the city before dark.

YOUNGER ANUNCIA. How long will we be gone?

MAMI. Don't know. The Perónistas are putting up a fight – but they won't last long. The Opposition's growing stronger.

YOUNGER ANUNCIA. Is it true? Perón's gone?

MAMI. Yes, but he'll be back. Men like him always come back, again and again. Ushered in with another military coup or some public riot. We'll lay low for now, up north, out of the city, and then get you out of this country before it all goes to hell.

(Another distant explosion.)

You'll be in France, far away from all of this. My beautiful ballerina, dancing with the Nice Opera Ballet. A dream come true. An expensive dream. It costs a lot to live abroad. Are you going to accept the money your father wants to give you?

YOUNGER ANUNCIA. No.

MAMI. Now that the Governor's offices are closed, I'm out of work –

YOUNGER ANUNCIA. I can pay my own way. I'm making money of my own now –

MAMI. I know, but –

OLDER/YOUNGER ANUNCIA. No.

YOUNGER ANUNCIA. I don't want to owe him anything.

MAMI. I understand. But I need you to be safe. Take his money –

Mi vida. Take his money. It was once mine.

[NO. 14 – THE STORY OF THAT MAN]

OLDER/YOUNGER ANUNCIA. *No.*

OLDER ANUNCIA. Mami never told me the story of That Man and the hurt he caused her. It was Tía who told me, years after Mami's death. Oh, Mami...my beautiful mystery. Some memories I can change and some I can't. Some memories punish me. But... If I could punish a memory – put a memory on trial for its sins, I would put the memory of That Man to the task! The anemones want to know who he was and what he did, don't you? It's not my story to tell. It's Mami's.

> *(As* **MAMI**, **GRANMAMA**, *and* **TÍA** *relate the story of* **THAT MAN**, *he appears. He's an elegant but dangerous rogue.)*

MAMI.
> HE WAS A GAMBLER.
> HE PLAYED THE TABLES.
> BUT IT WAS POKER
> THAT MADE HIS NAME.
> LIKE ANY GAMBLER,
> HE HAD A WEAKNESS.
> SOME SAY ADDICTION.
> HE COULDN'T FOLD AND LEAVE THE GAME.

GRANMAMA.
> HE WAS A ROUGH DOG.

TÍA.
> BUT SMOOTH AND HANDSOME.

MAMI.
> ASK ANY WOMAN.
> SHE'D SAY THE SAME.

MAMI, GRANMAMA & TÍA.
> LIKE ANY ROUGH DOG
> HE HAD A DARK SIDE.

GRANMAMA.
> SOME SAY A SCREW LOOSE.

MAMI, GRANMAMA & TÍA.
> AN APPETITE HE COULDN'T TAME.

MAMI.
> HE'D PRETEND HE DIDN'T SEE YOU.
> HE'D PRETEND HE DIDN'T WANT YOU.
> THEN HE'D CATCH YOUR EYE AND VANISH
> INTO THE CROWD.
> WHICH WOULD MAKE YOU NEED TO FIND HIM.
> YOU'D DO THINGS TO MAKE HIM WANT YOU.
> LIKE TOSSING YOUR HAIR
> WHILE FLIRTING WITH MEN
> AND LAUGHING TOO LOUD.

THEN HE'D GIVE YOU HIS SMILE
AND THAT ROUGH DOG WINK.
YOU WONDER WHAT I DID NEXT?
WHAT DO YOU THINK?
HA! I WAS A GAMBLER.

GRANMAMA & TÍA.
RECKLESS.

MAMI.
I TOOK MY CHANCES.

GRANMAMA & TÍA.
FOOLISH.

MAMI.
HE SAID HE LOVED ME.
NO THOUGHT OF SHAME.

GRANMAMA & TÍA.
CARMEN, CARMEN.

MAMI.
LIKE ANY GAMBLER,
I HAD A WEAKNESS.
HE SAID HE LOVED ME.
SO WHO'S AT FAULT
AND WHO'S TO BLAME?
FIRST THE MONEY FROM MY UNCLES.

GRANMAMA & TÍA.
GONE.

MAMI.
THEN THE SILVER FROM MY MOTHER.

GRANMAMA & TÍA.
SOLD.

MAMI.
THEN MY WEDDING RING AND JEWELRY.

GRANMAMA & TÍA.
> PAWNED.

>> (**MAMI** *now begins confronting* **THAT MAN** *directly.*)

MAMI.
> THEN THE KNOCKING ON THE DOOR
> IN THE MIDDLE OF THE NIGHT;
> MEN DEMANDING PAYMENTS.
> GRINNING WHILE THEY THREATENED:
> "WHAT WILL YOU GIVE US IN PLACE OF YOUR LIFE?
> MAYBE A GO AT YOUR SWEET LITTLE WIFE?
> LOOKS LIKE SHE'S PREGNANT – WHAT DO WE CARE?
> YOU MIGHT NEVER KNOW WHOSE CHILD SHE'LL BEAR."
> I'D NO MONEY FOR FOOD.
> YOU'D BE OUT PLACING BETS.
> UNTIL NOTHING WAS LEFT TO SETTLE YOUR DEBTS.

> Except...the house. Our house. The house my father
> bought for us when we got married. You lost our house
> in a bet!

> (*Confronting* **THAT MAN***:*) What are we going to do?
> Where will we live? Bastard! Where?! Where?!

>> (**THAT MAN** *slaps her. She returns the blow.*
>> *He raises his fists to begin pummeling her.*)

OLDER ANUNCIA. Stop!!

>> (**THAT MAN** *freezes, his fists in the air.*
>> **GRANMAMA** *and* **TÍA** *gather* **MAMI** *up and*
>> *hurry off.* **YOUNGER ANUNCIA** *remains.*
>> **OLDER ANUNCIA** *protectively stands in front*
>> *of her: a barrier between* **THAT MAN** *and the*
>> *girl.*)

> NO FORGIVENESS FOR YOU.
> NEVER.
> NO FORGIVENESS FOR YOU.

> (**THAT MAN** *turns toward* **OLDER ANUNCIA** *and begins to make a move, but* **OLDER ANUNCIA**, *with a gesture, stops him. She will control his actions from this point on, in a grotesque Apache, though neither one touches the other.*)

NO REDEMPTION FOR YOU.
EVER.
NO REDEMPTION FOR YOU.
I DO WHAT I WANT WITH YOU.
YOUR MEMORY, YOUR FACE.
I DO WHAT I WANT WITH YOU.
IGNORE.
FORGET.
DESTROY.
ERASE...

> (**THAT MAN** *and* **OLDER ANUNCIA** – *with* **YOUNGER ANUNCIA** *close behind her* – *circle each other.* **OLDER/YOUNGER ANUNCIA** *contorts* **THAT MAN**, *causing pain, punishing him. As the circle gets tighter and tighter, she makes him fall to his knees before her.*)

Here is the story I'll remember you by. I was five or six years old. We were on a trip somewhere in the north. You and I went ahead and Mami was going to join us the next day. We slept over in a little hotel –

OLDER/YOUNGER ANUNCIA. – in a room with two beds.

YOUNGER ANUNCIA. Mine was in the corner. Yours, against the opposite wall. That night I woke up to noises in the dark. I sat up and saw you in your bed, on top of a woman. She was making little crying sounds. It was not my mother. You turned and saw me looking at you and you smiled.

OLDER/YOUNGER ANUNCIA. You smiled at me and went back to your business.

OLDER ANUNCIA.

NO FORGIVENESS FOR YOU.

NEVER!

YOUNGER ANUNCIA.

NEVER!

OLDER/YOUNGER ANUNCIA. Never!!

(She banishes **THAT MAN,** *who flies away into the darkness, like a phantom.)*

OLDER ANUNCIA. I've only told Tía this story, and many years later, before she became ill. She asked me, maybe if I had dreamed it. She said, sometimes children dream things and they remember them as real things that happened. Is it possible to *imagine* a memory? Is it possible to create memories and after remembering them for so long, come to believe that they are true?

YOUNGER ANUNCIA. It was *not* a dream.

(A long beat.)

Come on. Get this done. You're purged. You're clean. Now you can let go.

OLDER ANUNCIA. Can I?

(**OLDER ANUNCIA** *picks up the box with Tía's ashes and holds it close.)*

Tía… During the last year, when I visited you, I'd read to you one of your favorite books.

[NO. 15 – LISTEN TO THE MUSIC (REPRISE)]

Sometimes I'd play you music that you liked and we'd sit together and listen, yes?

LISTEN TO THE MUSIC…

YOUNGER ANUNCIA.
TELL ME WHAT YOU'RE SEEING.

OLDER ANUNCIA.
LISTEN TO...

YOUNGER ANUNCIA.
...TO THE NOTES
AND LET THEM SWIRL AND DANCE
IN YOUR MIND.
THE PICTURES YOU FIND
ARE LITTLE SEEDS YOU CAN SOW.
LISTEN TO THE MUSIC
AND WATCH YOUR GARDEN GROW, GROW, GROW.

(To **OLDER ANUNCIA***:)* You're an orphan now. An orphan. That really scares you, doesn't it? It should. Because after you die, there'll be no one left to remember them. Now, dig a little deeper. Do it.

> *(***OLDER ANUNCIA*** digs a bit deeper into the hole she has dug.* **OLDER ANUNCIA** *feels something.)*

OLDER ANUNCIA. What is it?

> *(Slowly, she pulls out her missing left glove.)*

My other glove... But...how did...?

YOUNGER ANUNCIA. Magic realism. *(A beat.)* Do it. It's getting late and you have to drive back to New York, put on false eyelashes, and accept our Lifetime Achievement Award.

OLDER ANUNCIA. I don't want to go.

> *(***TÍA*** is packing some clothes into a box.* **YOUNGER ANUNCIA** *stops her.)*

YOUNGER ANUNCIA. I don't want to go. I'm not going to Europe.

TÍA. Of course you are. Everything's all arranged.

YOUNGER ANUNCIA. I don't care. I'm not going.

TÍA. This is an opportunity of a lifetime! We're all so happy for you!

YOUNGER ANUNCIA. I don't want to go. I can stay and continue working at the Teatro Colón. I like it there.

TÍA. I know. You could stay. But what good would that do for everyone else who'd miss out on your talent?

YOUNGER ANUNCIA. Who everyone else?

TÍA. The world!

YOUNGER ANUNCIA. You won't miss me.

TÍA. Now you're being silly. And narcissistic. *(A beat.)* You know you'd be safer abroad right now, far away from all the trouble.

YOUNGER ANUNCIA. But if I stay, I can help protect you.

TÍA. Protect us? With what? Your ballet shoes?

YOUNGER ANUNCIA. You just want me out of here.

TÍA. Yes, that is the truth. We simply can't have you around anymore. Teenagers are a nuisance.

YOUNGER ANUNCIA. Well, then. Goodbye to you.

TÍA. Don't be that way.

OLDER ANUNCIA. I do not want to be the *only one left*!

TÍA. We've done all we can do for you here. Look there, into the future: look at your garden. Look at the tomato blossoms. When a plant is in bloom, that's when it's most alive, before it bears fruit. You're in bloom now.

[NO. 16 – NEVER A GOODBYE]

It's time you announce yourself to the world. For me, Anuncia. And all the places I wanted to visit, all the adventures, all the pleasures to be had, all that I wanted to do, *you'll* do. All I wanted to show the world…*you'll* show the world.

OLDER ANUNCIA. How can I say goodbye?

YOUNGER ANUNCIA. How can I say goodbye to you?

> (**OLDER ANUNCIA** *takes the box filled with Tía's ashes and begins to bury it.*)

TÍA.
THERE IS NEVER A GOODBYE.
THERE IS NEVER A GOODBYE.
THERE IS NEVER A GOODBYE.
THERE IS ALWAYS A HELLO
FOR THE ONES WHO GIVE US LOVE.
FOR THE ONES WHO NEED OUR LOVE.
EVEN THOSE WHO WE LET GO.

WHILE I'M WISHING YOU GOODNIGHT,
I AM WISHING YOU GOOD MORNING.
I AM WISHING YOU
GARDENS OF TOMATOES AND SUMMER SQUASH.
KITCHENS FULL OF BUTTER AND BAKING BREAD.
HOUSES FILLED WITH MUSIC AND FAVORITE BOOKS
TO BE READ AND RE-READ.

I COULD NEVER SAY GOODBYE.
YOU COULD NEVER SAY GOODBYE.
WE COULD NEVER SAY GOODBYE.
YOU'RE AS MUCH A PART OF ME
AS I AM A PART OF YOU.
THERE IS NO DIVIDING UP
OR A CORD THAT CAN BE CUT.
THE PHENOMENON IS THIS:
THAT BEYOND A TOUCH OR KISS,
THAT BEYOND THIS LIFE WE KNOW,

WE WILL ALWAYS SAY HELLO.
AND FOR THOSE WHO WE LET GO:

TÍA.
THERE IS NEVER A GOODBYE.
THERE IS NEVER A GOODBYE.
THERE IS NEVER A GOODBYE.

> *(**OLDER ANUNCIA** has buried Tía's ashes. **YOUNGER ANUNCIA** vanishes. **MAMI**, **GRANMAMA** appear, and with **TÍA**, they call to **OLDER ANUNCIA**.)*

MAMI.
ANUNCIA!

MAMI & GRANMAMA.
ANUNCIA!

MAMI, GRANMAMA & TÍA.
ANUNCIA!

[NO. 17 – FINALE]

EVERY SUNDAY WE'LL WAKE UP EARLY.

OLDER ANUNCIA. *(To her garden.)* What else is there to tell you? What else would you like to know?

MAMI, GRANMAMA & TÍA.
MONDAY'S SCHOOL AND WE'LL HAVE TO HURRY.

OLDER ANUNCIA. Mami, who swore she would never marry again, married again and lived happily-ever-after.

MAMI, GRANMAMA & TÍA.
TUESDAY MORNING WE'LL START OUR CLEANING.

OLDER ANUNCIA. Granmama died when I was twenty, after I moved to America, where the only English word I knew was "okay."

MAMI, GRANMAMA & TÍA.
WEDNESDAY MORNING, WE'LL STILL BE CLEANING.

OLDER ANUNCIA. Tía's last words to me were *"¿Ves los pavos reales?"* "See the peacocks?"

MAMI, GRANMAMA & TÍA.
> THURSDAY NIGHT, WE'LL KNIT AND WE'LL SEW BY
> CANDLELIGHT.

OLDER ANUNCIA. Enough, Anuncia. You've got to put on false eyelashes and drive to the city and try to remember which people to thank.

MAMI, GRANMAMA & TÍA.
> FRIDAY'S HERE: WE'LL SIT ON THE LAWN DRINKING
> GINGER BEER.

OLDER ANUNCIA. I'll accept my award, take off my false eyelashes and drive right back here.

MAMI, GRANMAMA & TÍA.
> SATURDAY, WE'LL GO MARKET SHOPPING.

OLDER ANUNCIA. Maybe this weekend I'll invite my deer to watch the chipmunks tango.

MAMI, GRANMAMA & TÍA.
> SOMEHOW, WE SURVIVE AND IT'S SUNDAY.

OLDER ANUNCIA. My garden. It is not easy to keep you. I have to weed, aerate, fertilize, water, trim, weed some more – but you do the harder work. War and corruption, dictators, changing governments – that's nothing compared to what you're up against. Bugs and deer that want to eat you. Sudden cold snaps and heat waves. And you have to listen to this old woman rattle on with her stories and not-always-correct memories. I don't think you mind, though. I always thought it would be my art that I'd leave behind to be remembered by. It's not. It will be you.

> (**OLDER ANUNCIA** *sings to her mother, to her grandmother, to her aunt, to her grandfather, to her deer, to her anemones, to her peonies, to her tomatoes, to her garden, to us:*)

> THERE IS NEVER A GOODBYE.
> THERE IS NEVER A GOODBYE.

OLDER ANUNCIA.
>THERE IS NEVER A GOODBYE.
>THERE IS ALWAYS A HELLO.
>FOR THE ONES WHO GIVE US LOVE.
>FOR THE ONES WHO NEED OUR LOVE.
>EVEN THOSE WHO WE LET GO.
>
>WHILE I'M WISHING YOU GOODNIGHT,
>I AM WISHING YOU GOOD MORNING.

OLDER ANUNCIA & MAMI.
>I AM WISHING YOU
>GARDENS OF TOMATOES AND SUMMER SQUASH.

OLDER ANUNCIA, MAMI & GRANMAMA.
>KITCHENS FULL OF BUTTER AND BAKING BREAD.

OLDER ANUNCIA, MAMI, GRANMAMA & TÍA.
>HOUSES FILLED WITH MUSIC AND FAVORITE BOOKS
>TO BE READ AND RE-READ.

OLDER ANUNCIA. *Gracias*, Granmama. *Gracias*, Mami. *Gracias*, Tía. *Gracias*, my garden. You dirt, you weeds, you forsythia, you anemones, you tomatoes. All things waiting to bloom. *¡Gracias!*

MAMI.
>YOU'RE AS MUCH A PART OF ME
>AS I AM A PART OF YOU.

MAMI & TÍA.
>THERE IS NO DIVIDING UP

MAMI, GRANMAMA & TÍA.
>OR A CORD THAT CAN BE CUT.

MAMI, GRANMAMA & TÍA, GRANPAPA & DEER.
>THE PHENOMENON IS THIS:
>THAT BEYOND A TOUCH OR KISS,
>THAT BEYOND THIS LIFE WE KNOW –

TÍA.
WE WILL ALWAYS SAY HELLO.

OLDER ANUNCIA.
AND FOR THOSE WHO WE LET GO:
THERE IS NEVER A GOODBYE.
THERE IS NEVER A GOODBYE.
THERE IS NEVER A GOODBYE.

> (**MAMI**, **GRANMAMA**, **TÍA**, **GRANPAPA**, *and the* **DEER** *have disappeared into the garden.* **OLDER ANUNCIA** *follows them. Silence, but for the sound of birds and a breeze stirring the hedges.)*

The End

[NO. 18 – BOWS/EXIT MUSIC]